**STAND UP: Bullying Prevention**

# Smartphone BULLYING

Addy Ferguson

PowerKiDS press
New York

Published in 2015 by The Rosen Publishing Group, Inc.
29 East 21st Street, New York, NY 10010

Copyright © 2015 by The Rosen Publishing Group, Inc.

All rights reserved. No part of this book may be reproduced in any form without permission in writing from the publisher, except by a reviewer.

First Edition

Editor: Jennifer Way
Book Design: Erica Clendening and Colleen Bialecki
Book Layout: Andrew Povolny
Photo Research: Katie Stryker

Photo Credits: Cover Alistair Berg/Iconica/Getty Images; p. 5 Robert Mandel/Thinkstock; p. 6 Antonio_Diaz/iStock/Thinkstock; p. 7 Maxx-Studio/Shutterstock.com; p. 8 RimDream/Shutterstock.com; p. 9 Libra_photo/Thinkstock; p. 10 Monkeybusinessimages/iStock/Thinkstock; p. 11 Creatas/Thinkstock; p. 12 Kamira/Shutterstock; p. 13 Artistan/iStock/Thinkstock; p. 14 jeangill/E+/Getty Images; p. 15 Richard Gardette/iStock/Thinkstock; p. 17 moodboard/Thinkstock; p. 18 kitty/Shutterstock.com; p. 19 Photos.com/Thinkstock; p. 20 David Sacks/Photodisc/Thinkstock; p. 21 wavebreakmedia/iStock/Thinkstock; p. 22 Aigars Reinholds/Shutterstock.com.

Library of Congress Cataloging-in-Publication Data

Ferguson, Addy.
 Smartphone bullying / by Addy Ferguson. — First Edition.
    pages cm. — (Stand up: bullying prevention)
 Includes index.
 ISBN 978-1-4777-6888-4 (library binding) — ISBN 978-1-4777-6889-1 (pbk.) —
ISBN 978-1-4777-6624-8 (6-pack)
 1. Cyberbullying. 2. Cyberbullying—Prevention. I. Title.
 HV6773.15.C92F47 2015
 302.34'3—dc23
                                   2013049601

Manufactured in the United States of America

CPSIA Compliance Information: Batch #WS14PK5: For Further Information contact Rosen Publishing, New York, New York at 1-800-237-9932

# Contents

The Bullying Problem ............................................. 4
What Is Smartphone Bullying? ............................. 6
After the Bullying Ends .......................................... 8
Don't Engage the Bully ........................................ 10
Protect Yourself .................................................... 12
Find a Trusted Adult ............................................ 14
Report Smartphone Bullying ............................... 16
Who Gets Bullied? ................................................ 18
Technology Is a Tool ............................................ 20
Stopping Bullying Everywhere ............................ 22
Glossary ................................................................ 23
Index ..................................................................... 24
Websites ............................................................... 24

# The Bullying Problem

Bullying is repeatedly **taunting**, **excluding**, or hurting another person. A bully may say mean things every day. He may push the other person or make threats. A bully may convince other people to join in the bullying, too.

Bullying has always been around. Today, though, there are new ways to bully that your parents did not experience. People can use **technology** to bully. They can send emails or post things on the Internet to hurt another person. People can even use their smartphones to bully anywhere at any time of day.

Bullies can use computers to send hurtful emails or instant messages and to make bullying social media posts.

# What Is Smartphone Bullying?

We live in the age of the smartphone. It seems like everywhere you look, someone is texting, chatting, or sending emails using their phones. Smartphones are great tools for staying in touch or for making plans with friends.

Smartphones make people reachable by several methods. This can make it complicated to deal with smartphone bullying.

Smartphones let users make calls, send texts and emails, and connect with people using social media apps.

Some people use their smartphones for an uglier purpose, though. They use their phones to **cyberbully** others. People who use their smartphones to bully may send mean texts about a person. They may post false **rumors** on **social media** sites using their phones, too. The worst part is that bullying can happen even when you are not near the bully.

# After the Bullying Ends

No matter what form bullying takes, it feels bad. A person who is being bullied through technology may feel there is no way to avoid the bully. She may feel hopeless, **depressed**, angry, and scared. She may be embarrassed by the emails or posts the bully is writing about her.

When a bully targets people through their smartphones, they are able to read the bully's cruel words anytime and anywhere.

Kids who have been bullied may feel angry that they were singled out by the bully. These feelings are OK, but it is important to deal with them in a healthy way.

People who are bullied often suffer from low **self-esteem**. All these feelings do not go away easily. Some people start to do poorly in school or withdraw from activities. This can have an effect on the opportunities they pursue later in life.

# Don't Engage the Bully

You have probably been told before to walk away from someone who is bothering you. If you have, then you know it is hard to do. How do you do this when your bully targets you through a smartphone? If someone bullies you with a smartphone, do not respond.

It is really hard not to respond to a bully's texts. However, getting no upset response from you might bore the bully and cause her to leave you alone.

If a bully shares mean messages with you, don't share them with your friends. That would mean you are taking part in the bullying and showing that you think it is OK.

If someone sends you a bullying message about someone else, don't join in or spread bullying messages, either. Often, the person who bullies is looking for a reaction. If he does not get one, he might stop. If the attacks keep happening, still do not respond. It is time to ask for help.

# Protect Yourself

Saving bullying messages provides you with proof of the bullying.

The first thing you might want to do when you receive a bullying text or email is to delete it. However, it may be in your best interest to save it. You could archive it, print it, or forward it to a parent or trusted adult.

You can take a screenshot of social media pages where someone is bullying you or someone else, too. Save it in a folder and share it with a grown-up. Some software companies have made apps to help put a stop to cyberbullying. These apps let the user document harmful bullying activity and report it.

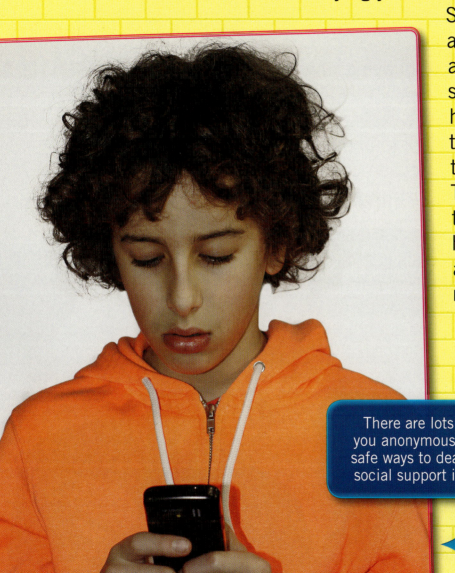

There are lots of apps that can help you anonymously report bullying, learn safe ways to deal with bullying, and get social support if you are being bullied.

# Find a Trusted Adult

As with any kind of bullying, the person being bullied often feels alone. He may feel like there is no point in telling anyone because no one can help. It is important to find someone to talk to about the problem, though. A parent, teacher, or coach could help the person being bullied come up with **strategies** for stopping the behavior.

A kid who is being targeted by a bully might talk to her parents and a teacher or counselor to discuss how to deal with the situation.

Telling a friend may help the bullied child feel better, too. However, it is still a good idea to get some adult support. The adult will have ideas for ways to make things better.

Talking to a friend might not help you find a way to stop the bullying. Friends are a good source of emotional support, though.

# Report Smartphone Bullying

When a person is being bullied with a smartphone, it is important for her to report it. If it is happening over text or email, the person should alert the service provider. If it is happening on a social media site, the **administrators** of that site should be alerted.

Bullying violates the **terms of service** of many sites, cell carriers, and apps. It's important to report it so the bully can be stopped. Very serious threats and abuse should be reported to the police.

> A parent can help you find the correct channels to report smartphone bullying.

# Who Gets Bullied?

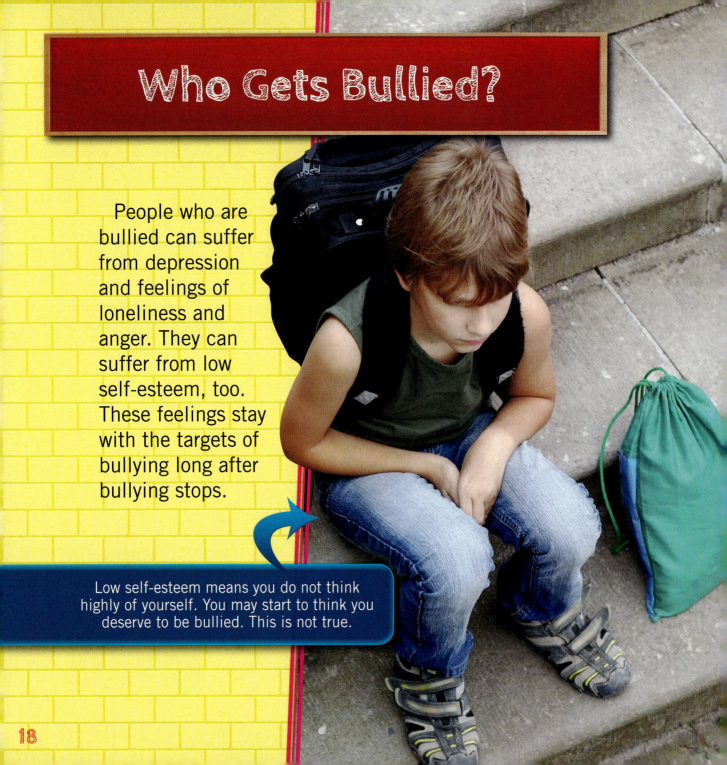

People who are bullied can suffer from depression and feelings of loneliness and anger. They can suffer from low self-esteem, too. These feelings stay with the targets of bullying long after bullying stops.

Low self-esteem means you do not think highly of yourself. You may start to think you deserve to be bullied. This is not true.

If you or someone you know is being bullied, it is important to talk to someone. An adult may be able to suggest a counselor to help you deal with your feelings. The school guidance counselor is a great resource as well. The most important thing to remember is that bullying is not your fault and you do not deserve it.

> Talking about your feelings can be difficult. Remember that your parents love you and want to know what is happening so they can help you.

# Technology Is a Tool

Technology can be a wonderful tool. It has changed the way people use, share, and access information. It should not be used as a weapon, though. Parents should be kept in the loop about what you are doing online and on your phone.

Some parents allow their kids to use computers and smartphones only in common areas of the home. This lets parents monitor how their kids use these devices.

Some tablets have many of the same functions as smartphones. It is a good idea for parents to watch how their kids use these devices, too.

If someone is bullying using a smartphone, he needs to be stopped. Being bullied is not the fault of the target. She should not feel she needs to hide what is happening. Adults are there to help you stay safe and use technology safely.

# Stopping Bullying Everywhere

The growing access kids have to technology means there are more ways to bully others. Just like bullying that happens on the playground or school bus, smartphone bullying should be stopped. If you know it is happening to someone else, stand up and say stop.

If it is happening to you, tell people about it. You will be surprised how many people will join you in trying to stop the bullying. No one deserves to be bullied.

Now that you know more about smartphone bullying, you can do your part to make others aware of this problem.

# Glossary

**administrators** (ed-MIH-neh-stray-terz) People who manage something.

**cyberbully** (SY-ber-bu-lee) To do hurtful or threatening things to other people using the Internet.

**depressed** (dih-PRESD) Being sad for a long time.

**excluding** (eks-KLOOD-ing) Leaving out.

**rumors** (ROO-murz) Stories that are heard by people with no proof that they are true.

**self-esteem** (SELF-uh-STEEM) Happiness with oneself.

**social media** (SOH-shul ME-dee-uh) Online tools that help people stay connected with one another.

**strategies** (STRA-tuh-jeez) Carefully made plans or methods.

**taunting** (TAWNT-ing) Repeated teasing with the purpose of hurting or upsetting someone.

**technology** (tek-NAH-luh-jee) Advanced tools that help people do and make things.

**terms of service** (TERMZ UV SER-vus) Rules which one must agree to follow to use a service.

# Index

**A**
adult(s), 11, 12, 15, 19, 21
apps, 13, 16

**B**
bully, 4, 7–8, 10, 16

**E**
email(s), 4, 6, 8, 12, 16

**F**
feelings, 9, 18–19
friend(s), 6, 15

**P**
parent(s), 4, 12, 14, 20

**S**
self-esteem, 9, 18
smartphone(s), 4, 6–7, 10, 16, 21

social media site(s), 7, 16
strategies, 14

**T**
teacher, 14
technology, 4, 8, 20–22
terms of service, 16
text(s), 7, 12, 16
threats, 4, 16
tool(s), 6, 20

# Websites

Due to the changing nature of Internet links, PowerKids Press has developed an online list of websites related to the subject of this book. This site is updated regularly. Please use this link to access the list: www.powerkidslinks.com/subp/phone/